This item is ~~~~~
from the

Friends of the Danville Library

Dear Parents and Educators,

Welcome to Penguin Young Readers! As parents and educators, you know that each child develops at his or her own pace—in terms of speech, critical thinking, and, of course, reading. Penguin Young Readers recognizes this fact. As a result, each Penguin Young Readers book is assigned a traditional easy-to-read level (1–4) as well as a Guided Reading Level (A–P). Both of these systems will help you choose the right book for your child. Please refer to the back of each book for specific leveling information. Penguin Young Readers features esteemed authors and illustrators, stories about favorite characters, fascinating nonfiction, and more!

| A Is for Amber | LEVEL **3** |
| Get Ready for Second Grade, Amber Brown | GUIDED READING LEVEL **K** |

This book is perfect for a **Transitional Reader** who:
- can read multisyllable and compound words;
- can read words with prefixes and suffixes;
- is able to identify story elements (beginning, middle, end, plot, setting, characters, problem, solution); and
- can understand different points of view.

Here are some **activities** you can do during and after reading this book:
- Compound Words: A compound word is made when two words are joined together to form a new word. *Notebook* is a compound word that is used in this story. Reread the story and find other compound words.
- Make Connections: In this book, we learn that amber comes from tree sap that gets hard. We also learn that "amber" is the Greek word for *electron*. What makes your name special? Do you share your name with someone else you know?

Remember, sharing the love of reading with a child is the best gift you can give!

—Bonnie Bader, EdM
   Penguin Young Readers program

*Penguin Young Readers are leveled by independent reviewers applying the standards developed by Irene Fountas and Gay Su Pinnell in *Matching Books to Readers: Using Leveled Books in Guided Reading*, Heinemann, 1999.

To the Salwens—Peter, Peggy, James,
and William—with love—PD

To Laura—TR

Penguin Young Readers
Published by the Penguin Group
Penguin Group (USA) Inc., 375 Hudson Street, New York, New York 10014, USA
Penguin Group (Canada), 90 Eglinton Avenue East, Suite 700, Toronto, Ontario M4P 2Y3, Canada
(a division of Pearson Penguin Canada Inc.)
Penguin Books Ltd., 80 Strand, London WC2R 0RL, England
Penguin Group Ireland, 25 St. Stephen's Green, Dublin 2, Ireland (a division of Penguin Books Ltd.)
Penguin Group (Australia), 250 Camberwell Road, Camberwell, Victoria 3124, Australia
(a division of Pearson Australia Group Pty. Ltd.)
Penguin Books India Pvt. Ltd., 11 Community Centre, Panchsheel Park, New Delhi—110 017, India
Penguin Group (NZ), 67 Apollo Drive, Rosedale, Auckland 0632, New Zealand
(a division of Pearson New Zealand Ltd.)
Penguin Books (South Africa) (Pty.) Ltd., 24 Sturdee Avenue,
Rosebank, Johannesburg 2196, South Africa

Penguin Books Ltd., Registered Offices: 80 Strand, London WC2R 0RL, England

Text copyright © 2002 by Paula Danziger. Illustrations copyright © 2002 by Tony Ross. All rights reserved.
First published in 2002 by G. P. Putnam's Sons and in 2003 by Puffin Books, imprints of
Penguin Group (USA) Inc. Published in 2012 by Penguin Young Readers, an imprint of
Penguin Group (USA) Inc., 345 Hudson Street, New York, New York 10014. Manufactured in China.

The Library of Congress has cataloged the Putnam edition under
the following Control Number: 2001019713

ISBN 978-0-14-250081-1   10 9 8 7 6 5

ALWAYS LEARNING   PEARSON

IS FOR AMBER

Get Ready for Second Grade, Amber Brown

by Paula Danziger
illustrated by Tony Ross

Penguin Young Readers
An Imprint of Penguin Group (USA) Inc.

Much thanks to
Sheryl Hardin and her Brainy Bunch at
Gullett Elementary School 2000–2001

Jacob Backhaus	Alex Manulik
Ashley Calhoun	Frances Mayo
Amber Day	Simon McCann
Neal Edmondson	Jordyn Michalik
Kelly Ellis	Madalyn Montgomery
Gregory Gomez	Kristin Page
Will Grover	Kate Van Dyke
Danielle Johnson	Victor Vogt
Kramer Jones	Kelly Wray

The good news is that I, Amber Brown,

am going to be a second-grader.

The bad news is that Mrs. Wilson,

the second-grade teacher,

had to quit two weeks ago.

Her husband got a new job

and they moved.

Anyone who was ever a second-grader

LOVED Mrs. Wilson and said she was

a great teacher.

She used to smile at me in the hall.

Now there's going to be a new teacher.

I don't know her.

She doesn't know me.

What if she doesn't like me?

I try not to think about it.

In just an hour I will find out

who the second-grade teacher is.

Right now I will get ready for school.
On my bed are all my school
supplies: new pens and pencils,
a new notebook, and my lucky pen
with purple feathers.

I unzip my new teddy-bear backpack.

My aunt Pam sent it to me.

She said that it's an

"Enjoy Second Grade Present."

I named him Bear Lee.

His full name is Bear Lee Brown

because he is barely brown, and he

is barely ready for second grade.

Just like me.

I put everything in my backpack
and zip it up.

"Bear Lee," I say, "you are so special.

Everyone is going to like you

except Hannah Burton.

But don't worry.

She is mean to a lot of people,

especially me."

"Amber," my mom calls upstairs.

"It's time for breakfast."

I pick up Bear Lee and look

in the mirror.

I'm wearing my new clothes.

On my knee is a scab.

It is almost ready to fall off.

I named it Scabulous.

Bear Lee, Scabulous, and I are ready.

Second grade, here we come!

Breakfast.

Mom and Dad have breakfast with me.

"You look beautiful," Dad says.

I smile at him.

"You look smart," he continues.

"You look like everybody will want you

to be their best friend."

Mom puts a bowl of cereal

in front of me.

"I know that this is going to be

a great year for you," she says.

I, Amber Brown, know that they are

just saying that because they are my

mom and dad.

There's a knock on the door.

It's Justin, my best friend.

He is wearing his new

Roboman backpack.

15

My dad is driving Justin and
me to school.
Justin says, "This year
I am going to tell chicken jokes."
I just look at him.

"Why did the chicken

cross the playground?" he asks.

I think about it.

"To get to second grade?"

He makes a face.

"No, silly.

To get to the other slide."

My father laughs and so do I.

We get out of the car and go to
the playground.
That's where second-graders meet
before school starts.
Jimmy Russell and Bobby Clifford
are wrestling on the ground
in their brand-new school clothes.

Vinnie Simmons is showing everyone
the snake tattoo on his arm.
Even though he tells everyone it is
real, I can tell that it's not.

I stick my finger in my mouth
to get it wet.
I ask Vinnie to let me look
at the tattoo.
I touch it with my wet finger.

Some of it comes off.

I don't say anything, but I, Amber
Brown, know for sure that the tattoo
is not on Vinnie's arm forever.

Vinnie knows I know.

He sticks out his tongue at me.

Gregory Gifford and Freddie Romano
are showing each other the tricks that
they have learned over the summer.
Gregory can whistle, standing on
his hands.
Freddie can recite 15 state
capitals and do armpit music
at the same time.

The girls are talking about the
new teacher.

Alicia Sanchez says that her name
is Ms. Light.

"I hear that she really wants to teach
high-school students," Alicia says.

"I hear that she calls second-graders
'knee biters,'" Naomi Schwartz adds.

Tiffany Schroeder holds on to her
good-luck Barbie doll.

"I'm scared," she says.

"I want Mrs. Wilson to come back."

Hannah Burton joins our group.

She looks at my backpack.

"How baby, Amber.

A second-grader shouldn't wear a

baby backpack that looks like a

teddy bear."

I am not going to let Hannah
ruin second grade for me.
I ignore Hannah Burton.
Naomi and Alicia put their animal
backpacks down next to Bear Lee
and look at Hannah.
She shrugs and mumbles, "Babies."

My class talks about Ms. Light and
the things that we are worried about.
I wasn't so worried until we all
started talking.
What if she gives seven hours of
homework?

What if she gets really upset
if we color outside the lines?

What if she doesn't give out
bathroom passes?

What if she's an alien from some
foreign planet?

The bell rings.

It's time to meet Ms. Light.

We all go inside to Room 2.

Ms. Light doesn't look like any teacher

I've ever seen before.

She looks like a high-school kid

or a babysitter.

She's wearing a denim dress.

There are all sorts of patches

and pins on it—school buses, pens,

pencils, chalk, books, paper . . .

She's got on earrings

that are shaped like lightbulbs . . .

and they light up.

I get it . . . Ms. Light.

Lightbulbs.

She smiles and says
"Hello" and "Welcome"
to each of us as we go in.
She even says hello to Bear Lee.
I'm beginning to think
that Ms. Light might be okay.

The entire room is decorated.
We go to the seats where our names
are written on cardboard
cutouts of lightbulbs.

I'm sitting with Fredrich Allen.
I hope that over the summer
he stopped picking his nose.

I'm sitting with Justin Daniels.

Hooray.

I'm sitting with Hannah Burton.

Yuck.

Hannah looks at my name
on the cardboard lightbulb.
"Amber Brown.
What a sap you are.
You probably don't even know
that amber comes from tree sap.
Sometimes there are things
like spiders and bugs in it."
I know she is right about that.
My mom gave me a book about
amber, and my dad gave me an
amber pendant with
a little fly in it.
Hannah makes
a face at me.
That's it.

I say, "Look, Hannah BURPton.

Stop it."

Fredrich Allen says,

"Hannah Burpton."

Justin starts singing,

"Unhappy Burpton to you."

Ms. Light stands at the front
of the room.

"Welcome to second grade,"
she says and smiles at us.

"This is going to be such
an exciting school year.

We are going to learn new things
about the world and ourselves."

She continues,

"As you know, my name is Ms. Light.

Do you know what the word *light*

means?"

I raise my hand quickly.

I want to be the first person

to answer a question in second grade.

Everyone else has a hand raised.

Ms. Light chooses Fredrich.

"Light is a kind of energy," he says.

Fredrich Allen is very smart.

Ms. Light beams at him.

I guess that makes it a Light beam.

She says, "Absolutely right.

Light helps us to see things.

Most of our light comes from the sun.

Some of our light comes from

the moon.

We get light from electricity

when we flick a switch."

Justin pretends to put his finger

in a make-believe socket.

"ZZZZZZZZZZing."

Ms. Light nods at him.

"That can really happen . . .

electricity can be very powerful."

"Wow," we all say.

She grins at me.

"Amber.

Do you know what your name has to

do with the word

electricity?"

I shake my

head no.

She continues, "The word *electricity* comes from the word *electron.* Electricity is flowing electrons. The Greek word for *electron* is . . ."

Everyone looks at me.

"Amber," Ms. Light says.

I light up.

I, Amber Brown, am so happy.

I guess now that I know about
electricity, I can say that I am all
charged up.

Turning to Justin, I grin.

He gives me a thumbs-up.

"Way to go."

I look at Hannah Burton.

I smile and cross my eyes.

Ms. Light continues, "I want all of
you to have lots of energy to learn
and to grow.

I, Ms. Light, want to help you shine
as students.

From now on, you are going
to be the group known as
the Bright Lights."
We all grin.

Next, Ms. Light gives us all the rules
we will follow in second grade.

We will be respectful.

We will be on time.

We will do our work.

Then she picks up a book from her

desk and goes to her rocking chair.

She starts reading us a book.

It's a chapter book.

Hooray!

By the end of the year, I, Amber Brown, am going to be able to read a chapter book all on my own.

And next year, when I go to third grade, I'm going to tell the new second-graders that they don't have to be scared.

I, Amber Brown, am ready for second grade.